Obi

Seminole Maroon Freedom Fighter

by Martha R. Bireda

Illustrated by Anne Shively

blue ocean press

To Joyce:
Stay free!
Martha R. Bireda

Published by:

blue ocean press, an Imprint of ARI
#807-36 Lions Plaza Ebisu
3-25-3 Higashi, Shibuya-ku
Tokyo, Japan 150-0011

Email: contact@blueoceanpublications.com
URL: http://www.blueoceanpublications.com

ISBN: 978-4-902837-03-2

Contents

Dedicated to the brave men and women who resisted, rebelled against enslavement, and established communities based upon African values; The African Seminole Maroons You are true heroes and heroines.

Foreword

The story of the Black Maroon/Black Seminole in Florida symbolizes one of the purest examples of American freedom. As we learn more about these people during their time in Florida, we discover a deeper understanding of what it means to be free. Black Seminoles display a quest for the freedom of self expression and cultural awareness. Their time in Florida can be viewed in three phrases.

The development of the community is considered to be Phase 1of their history in Florida. It begins in the early 16th century with a known relationship between Africans and Native Americans. Both groups resisted slavery and plantation society. The Native Americans encouraged Africans to leave and live in the forest with them.

Phase 2 begins in the mid-seventeenth (17th) century. As the English invaded Florida, the competition for African labor increased. Africans continued to resist within plantation society by creating their own culture called Gullah. By the late 17th century, many of these Gullah people began to leave the English plantation system in search of promised freedom in Florida. Maroon societies began to grow, prosper and thrive in Florida during the 18th century. Native Americans were being infused into Gullah culture and vice versa. The Gullah language changed into the Afro Seminole Creole language in Florida. They developed further into the Black Seminoles.

Phase 3 signifies the fall and removal of the Maroon societies and Black Seminoles. Florida was slowly changing from a Spanish Territory to a member of the United States. This change was met with three Wars. The First Seminole War, cleared the way for Florida to become a United States territory. The Second Seminole War, (which is considered the most deadly of all Indian Wars) removed all but a few small maroon societies or Black Seminole villages. As a result, Florida became the 27th state in the -United States. The Black Seminoles were removed from Florida but it was seen as a great victory because they earned their freedom in Oklahoma.

Although Obi is a fictional character, he demonstrates all of the cultural mannerisms of the Florida maroon, his quest for freedom was also their quest. The story of Obi's freedom is not only a Floridian story but also an American story of freedom.

Map Of the Southern Underground Railroad

John's Island, South Carolina
to Central Florida.
Then to Texas and Mexico

Introduction

You are about to embark on a wonderful journey through history. As you read the story, use your imagination, see and feel what life was like 200 years ago. Take this journey with "Jack", a young man your age who was enslaved on a South Carolina plantation. Travel with Jack as he escapes from enslavement, and takes the daring and dangerous trip to freedom.

You will take the same journey as taken by a very special group of people. These people were called "Maroons". Maroons were Africans who escaped from enslavement and established their own free communities. Maroons were able to continue to practice many of their African cultural practices.

The word "maroon" comes from the Spanish word "cimarrón" originally used to refer to cattle that took to the hills of Hispaniola. Soon after it was used to describe Indian slaves who escaped from the Spanish on that island, and then to Africans who ran away and formed their own settlements. The word "maroon" can also mean being "fierce", "wild" or "untamed".

Maroon communities were established in every area in which slavery existed. Maroon communities existed in the Caribbean, South America, Central America, and North America. In the United States, the most successful maroon communities were found in the Great Dismal Swamp, on the border between North Carolina and Virginia, in Louisiana, and in Florida.

The group of Maroons that you will be reading about in this book is the African Seminole Maroons. These Africans mostly the "Gullah", escaped from South Carolina and Georgia to Florida. They became allies with the Seminole Indians, established their own free settlements, and fought in wars to keep their freedom.

As you take this journey with Jack, you will see him transformed from a fearful young man in bondage, to a courageous risk-taker who becomes "Obi" the Maroon, and finally Obi, the leader of a Maroon settlement.

Now get ready to share the heart-pounding danger that Jack and his friends experienced as they take the perilous trip to freedom.

"The "Learnings"

Life for young men and women who became maroons was filled with danger. The first risk that they took was escaping from the plantation and making it safely to freedom. Once in the maroon village, they had to constantly be on guard for slave catchers and militia who would attack their villages and attempt to return them to slavery.

The two most important concerns of the maroons were their freedom and safety. Both young men and women had to learn how to protect the freedom and safety of the settlement. Young men were taught to be warriors and to defend the women and children from harm. Young woman were taught how to plant and harvest crops as well as how to be prepared to move their food and belongings to a safe place when danger was near.

Young men and women in maroon communities had to learn many lessons. They had to sit with the elders to learn about the African traditions, what was expected of them as maroons, and most importantly, how to protect their freedom. These lessons were called "the learnings". The learnings are powerful teachings that helped the young maroons to develop the skills and traits that would ensure their freedom. We can think of the skills as what the young people were taught to "do"; and the traits as how they were to "be". For instance, skills that were learned might be to how to plan a successful escape, to survive in the forest, or how to establish a new village; while traits that were important to develop were patience, self-discipline, and the ability to persist in the face of obstacles.

In this story, through the learnings, Obi developed the skills and traits which helped him successfully escape to freedom, and to become a leader of his people. Among the skills that Obi learned was how to plan, set goals, and problem-solve. He became determined to have his freedom, and aware of his gift as a leader. Most importantly, Obi learned to liberate his mind from the stereotypes that would limit his beliefs about what was possible for him.

In order to survive in a new environment and to establish successful communities, Obi learned to form alliances with the Seminoles, to be creative, resourceful, and create strong bonds of unity and solidarity.

Now get ready to share the heart-pounding danger that Obi and his friends experienced as they take the perilous trip to freedom.

Acknowledgments

A special thanks to:

Dr. Sharon Whitehill for her guidance and brilliant instruction during this process.

The members of my writing group for their thoughtful criticism and inspiration:

Roxanne Hanney

Kay Kimball

Colleen Clopton

Peggydawn Moran

Lee Campbell

Myrna Charry

Sharon Whitehill

My daughter Saba for her helpful comments and encouragement, and my son Jaha for his willingness and assistance to me in developing this concept into a book.

Dr. Anthony Dixon, John Griffin, Scot and Jill Shively for their encouragement and support.

Anne Shively for her incredibly wonderful illustrations that capture the time and feeling of the story.

Prologue

The boys frantically dug up the bundles they'd buried under the rocks. Their hearts beat feverishly. Under the noses of their masters, they were walking away from enslavement. They were on their way to freedom. Earlier, they had bid a swift and secret goodbye to their families and walked down the streets of the quarter with fishing poles on their shoulders.

"How many fish will you catch today, Sam?" Toby hoped that his voice sounded teasing.

"Last week all he caught were those three tiny ones," mocked Jack. He was trembling inside but was determined that he wouldn't show it.

As they approached the end of the quarters' street, they spied the overseer. Their hearts pounded, their mouths went dry, and their legs weakened.

"Keep walking and talking", encouraged Jack in a whisper.

"What you boys up too?" inquired Roy, the overseer. His red leathery skin, frowning brow and creased neck made him appear even more menacing in this moment as when he was whipping a disobedient slave. Now he patted that same whip, which was hanging on his hip.

"Nutin massa, jus goin to try to catch some fish", answered Jack in a submissive tone that the slaves deliberately affected.

"What you got in that sack?" quizzed Roy as he walked toward them.

"Just some fatback for bait", volunteered Sam as he opened the sack.

"Okay, you boys get along; don't get into any mischief, you hear?"

"No sir, we won't," they all chimed as they walked away with heads bowed.

"Massa, I'm gon catch the biggest one I ever caught today!" laughed Sam, when they were out of earshot.

The moment they entered the woods just beyond the plantation, they began to feel like they were floating.

Though it was too soon to feel safe, they were filled with a lightness and energy they had never felt before. Around them, the world seemed transformed. The sky was the most tranquil and beautiful blue they had ever seen, and even the sun shining down seemed to surround them with a heavenly glow. Excitement mixed with their fear at the knowledge that they were embarking on the most dangerous plan of their lives. The past risks they had taken—such as "liberating" a chicken or two, or feigning sickness to catch up on sleep—felt like child's play. And before long they were running, skipping, leaping, and clapping. Again and again they all shouted these magical words: "We're on our way! We're finding our freedom! We're going to be free!"

But when they entered the thick, heavy woods the mood suddenly altered. Jack stopped short. "Did you hear that?" he demanded.

They crowded around him. "Hear what? I didn't hear nothin'."

"Shush. Let me listen. I thought I heard voices."

"Is it dogs? Oh dickens! Run! Run!"

And before Jack could stop them they were off, propelling themselves through the thickets, briars, and running vines until their chests hurt too much to go on.

Scratched, bleeding, breathless, they collapsed on the forest floor.

"Calm down!" Jack panted. "It was nothing. No one has any idea yet that we're even gone. We have to remember our learnings!"

At his words, the thought of Quashee's stern and scowling face jumped into all of their minds. They remembered his words." Become invisible, become one with the forest." This calmed their fears and renewed their confidence in the learnings. It was sobering to realize that only an hour into the journey to freedom, their perilous travels barely begun, they had panicked already. It would be a wonder if they succeeded.

The African

One late afternoon, Jack sneaked off to the pond to
go fishing and caught six big fish. The sun was going down
by the time he must hurry back to the quarters. Smiling to
himself, he gathered the fish, picked up his pole, and was
turning to leave, when he almost jumped out of his skin.
Standing behind him, a tall black man seemed to appear
out of nowhere.

He had neither heard nor felt the man approaching. But now he dropped both his pole and his fish and backed away. Too startled even to run, he felt numb. All he could do was stand trembling, his pounding heart surely audible to the stranger. Why didn't the man say or do something?

As he stared, Jack noticed his buckskin leggings, moccasins, and a beaded sash worn across the left shoulder of a shirt that reached almost to his knees. On his right shoulder a beaded pouch hung, and four pieces of silver, shaped like moons, dangled from his neck. Two silver bracelets completed his unusual costume.

What was he seeing? Jack's mind raced. Here was a man black as he was—yet utterly different. What were those lines drawn on his face? Most shocking, he had a weapon. A weapon! Jack knew very well that slaves couldn't have weapons. If Jack's muscles hadn't felt frozen, he would have reached out and touched this apparition.

For what seemed more endless a time than waiting to catch a rabbit or squirrel, he gazed at the man. His thoughts buzzed. "Who is he? *What* is he? Can he be a slave like me? Why is he here?"

The dark piercing eyes gazed back at him. Then the man spoke in a voice surprisingly gentle. "I am Quashee. I have traveled from Florida with my Seminole brothers. We come to tell you how you can be free."

Free? Despite the sudden lump in his throat, Jack forced out the words. "I am Jack."

The African shook Jack's hand. "Yes," he smiled, "I have come to speak to you of freedom. Because I, too, was once enslaved on a cotton plantation as you are now. But I ran away, to Florida, traveling many days and nights through swamps to avoid the slave catchers."

Jack's own dark eyes opened wider. "Then what?"

"I heard that if I could reach and cross the river called St. Mary into Florida, I would be free. When I finally arrived, I was befriended by Seminole Indians. They took me to their village, and gave me food and I met the Micco or Seminole chief. He made me an offer that I could not refuse.

"We can be of help to each other," he offered, "If you come under my protection, or become my slave in name only, you are protected by law from the slave catchers. Legally, you cannot be sent back to your master in South Carolina."

"I thought, wow! "What do I have to do in return?" I asked.

"We need only be brothers in the fight to protect both our land and your freedom. If you will join us in fighting against our enemies we will protect you. And each year if you give me a small tribute or amount of what you grow, that will be sufficient."

In his eagerness to hear more, Jack found himself moving closer to the African. "Do you live with the Indians? Why did they even *call* you a slave if you weren't?"

"It was just the word they used to indicate that the Seminole chief would protect me. I live near my Indian brothers. To them, it means nothing like what you might understand as being a slave. It means that I have my own village with others like me—slaves who have run away from white masters. We plant our own fields, we raise crops and stock. In return, once a year, we give the chief some of our products. But as you see"—here Quashee held up his musket and Jack's mouth fell open—"we own weapons like these. We need them to hunt and to defend ourselves from slave catchers. And we can travel wherever and whenever we please." He smiled. "I and my Seminole friends...we are equals."

Jack's could hardly believe what his two ears were hearing. An African, with a weapon, who is his own master? He had never imagined such a thing.

As if Quashee read his thoughts, he looked directly into Jack's eyes. "It is possible for you, too, you know." His voice was gentle. "You can be free. Just like me."

"But how? Tell me!"

"I will show you." Quashee held up a hand as if in warning. "But first, before any actions, you must have the learnings.

Jack was confused. As if in protest, he wrinkled his nose. "What are the learnings?"

"The learnings are all the ways you have to think and behave if you want to become free and keep your freedom. These are the lessons necessary for the success of your long, long journey to freedom. They are not easy lessons. But if you want to live free, never again to be enslaved, I must teach them to you." He paused, to let this sink in. "So gather your friends. Meet me in this place tomorrow night and we will begin the learnings. They are needed to take you to freedom."

Quashee turned to leave, then turned back. Jack's final surprise of the day was the flash of a grin on his fierce painted face. "Let this be a warning, Jack. *Never let yourself be surprised.*" Then, as quietly as he had come, he disappeared into the woods.

Fear of Freedom

Jack was so giddy, he jumped, skipped, and laughed all the way back to the quarters. He was too excited to sleep; his mind swirled with the African and what he had told him about being free. He imagined himself owning a farm, coming and going as he pleased, traveling without a pass, and having no fear of the lash. Each breath he took expanded his chest with an image of newfound freedom.

But the next day his excitement faded away as doubts and fears crept in. Thoughts of no more master or overseer clashed with worry about reaching Florida safely. How dumb could he be? What if he was caught? Why was he even listening to this strange African? On top of this, he recalled what that Aunt Sally told him a few days ago. "The master has noticed you," she had confided. "He thinks you might be trained as a servant in the big house." How overjoyed he had been to think he might leave hard work in the fields behind.

Over and over, as the day passed, Jack returned to the idea of being a house slave. He wouldn't be free, but his life would be better than now. He would wear better clothes and eat left-over foods from the master. Imagining this, he decided not to share with the others his encounter with the African. Instead he would return and tell Quashee that he had changed his mind.

But it was with real reluctance that Jack edged towards the woods to meet Quashee. He approached with his head down and eyes on the ground. And when he spoke, he stumbled over the words that did want to come out of his mouth. "Aunt Sally says the master wants me to be a house slave. That life will not be as bad as it is as a field slave. I'll get to wear better clothes and—"

Quashee's arms flew up in the air. His eyes narrowed. Anger clouded his face. "But you will still be a slave!" he exclaimed before Jack could go on. "You will not own your own life! You will not own even your name!" His eyes flashed. Then his voice grew more gentle. "Think of it, Jack. A bell will still wake you up in the morning so you can serve the master of the house. You might get to wear his cast-off clothes and eat his left-over food. But you still must walk with a bowed head. And you must never let your true feelings be known. Do you really want to that—answering to a master—for the rest of your life?"

By now tears were rolling down both of Jack's cheeks. Waiting for even more painful words from Quashee, he held his breath. All he could hear was his own thudding heart. Would Quashee strike him? He should never have dared to come back to explain.

But Quashee mastered himself. "What is it that you are afraid of?" he asked. "What makes you so afraid to seek freedom?"

"I don't want to leave my Aunt Sally?" Jack muttered. "I'd also have to leave all my friends behind." Then Jack heard what he had said about his friends and felt ashamed of his selfishness. He bowed his head. "I mean, I want to be free, but I don't know what to expect. I don't know what freedom is like. All I know is how to be a slave." His words began to pour out. "The master always tells us how horrible it is for slaves who run away. He says they usually starve because there's no master to give them food. He says we don't know how to take care of ourselves, or find our way North, or how not to be eaten by wild animals. Most of all, I'm afraid of what I've seen with my own eyes when slaves run away. They're always caught. And they're whipped. And some have their ears cut off, or even their legs!"

Quashee wrapped his big arm around Jack's trembling shoulders. "I understand these fears. At first, I too was afraid. But once I tasted my freedom, even during that long, hard journey to Florida, it was all I wanted. Freedom. That's what will happen to you, Jack. When you finish the learnings, you will be afraid no longer. Rather than be enslaved once again, you will fight to the death."

As Jack listened he felt his fear drain away. Courage began to build in his heart. Quashee the African *could* show him how to reach Florida safely—how to live free. That night, Jack made a vow. To himself he promised freedom. To Quashee he promised that he and his friends would come the next night to begin their learnings.

The Learnings Begin

Jack wondered what his best friends, Sam, Tom, John, and Toby, would say when he told them about the mysterious African with his promise of freedom. To his relief, they were eager to meet the man. Waiting until they knew that the overseer was asleep and the slave quarters quiet, they all slipped away into the woods at the edge of the plantation.

Ever mindful of the warning—*Never let yourself be surprised*—Jack kept a good watch, looking ahead, behind, and from side to side. Suddenly he saw an entire tree move. It was Quashee the African, covered from head to toe in leaves and moss. As he stepped out to greet the boys, they jumped back in amazement. "Now I have seen everything," thought Jack. He could only guess at the other boys' thoughts until he saw their faces, every bit as astonished as his own must be.

"Sit on the ground in a circle," Quashee said to the boys, who obeyed without saying a word.

"Why do you have those lines on your face? Toby ventured at last.

"These lines show which tribe I am from," rumbled Quashee. "In Africa I was a warrior. Before I was captured by an enemy tribe, that is, and sold to the slavers."

After several more questions like this, the boys grew impatient. Sam rocked back and forth, Tom twirled a small stick in a hole, John tapped rhythms out on a log. Finally Toby nudged Jack. "When are we going to talk about freedom?" he whispered.

As though he could read lips—or minds—Quashee mimicked his question. "Why are we here? Hasn't Jack told you about the learnings? What is their purpose?" The answer gushed from the mouths of the boys. "We want to be free like you!" they chorused.

Quashee smiled, nodding his head. "Yes, you want to be free. And the learnings will provide the way to freedom. But before you can become free like me, there are all kinds of things I must teach you."

Disappointed frowns greeted this statement. *You promised us freedom,* the frowns seemed to say. *But all you want to do is talk about 'learnings.'*

Now Quashee did a strange thing. "Close your eyes," he instructed. "See yourself in your mind. Tell me what you see."

The boys obeyed, closing their eyes. But not before rolling them.

"I see myself standing in the cotton field," Toby said.

"I see myself closing the gate so the cows won't escape." This was Sam.

The rest imagined themselves in slightly different settings. But every one of them pictured himself in bare feet and shabby clothes. All were still slaves.

"Exactly!" Quashee slapped a fist in his palm. "Right now, you can't see beyond slavery. And only when you see yourself free will you be ready for freedom." Quashee nodded and lowered his voice. "That is the purpose of the learnings: to make you ready for freedom."

"I get it," said Jack. "We can't free our bodies from slavery until our minds can think free."

"Yes. Understand that. Freedom must be all there is. Rather than facing enslavement again, you would choose death. And so today's learning is about freeing your mind—when you can free yourself from identifying yourself as a slave."

Quashee leaned back on his heels to let this sink in. Then he spread his hands toward the boys as if making an offering. "You must remove from your mind all of the lies you've been told about Africans by the master. You have been taught that you are inferior, stupid, and helpless—that you deserve to be enslaved. When your mind is free, you will accept such lies no longer."

The boys shifted in their seats, never having heard talk like this before.

"To be free," Quashee went on, "you must know your true selves. Who are you truly? Not the false, fawning selves that the master has taught you to see." Quashee rubbed his hands together as if washing them clean. "Every such image or picture must be removed. Only when you have the true image of who you are in your minds , will you be ready to liberate your bodies from slavery." He paused, then finished softly, "Then you will be ready to become freedom seekers."

The boys were all still and silent as statues.

Quashee leaned down and looked deeply into the eyes of each one. "Are you ready to become free? Can you make a commitment to freedom such as I have described? Are you willing to do the work of becoming free?"

The boys' faces shone as if lit from inside. In silence, and with their eyes only, each one confirmed his pledge to learn to be free.

Satisfied, Quashee straightened. As boys stood up, he patted each one on the shoulder. "I have other plantations to visit. I will see you again in one week."

And with that, the walking, talking tree that was Quashee disappeared into the night.

$500 Reward
Run Away House Servant

Goes by name of George. Wearing green jacket, red vest, and gray breeches. Dressed very well. 5ft 10 tall, chestnut brown skin, speckled gray hair. Very clever and deceitful. A known liar. Has an undated pass. May claim to be free. Disappeared in Savannah. I will pay the above reward for the apprehension and return of this scoundrel. B. Silcox, Subscriber

The friends raced through the woods so fast that their feet were a blur. Their hearts pulsed and their minds overflowed with excitement. Although the master had forbidden any house slave to tell, the secret was bubbling through the quarters like a fast stream: the master's most trusted servant had run away!

Confused and upset, the master simply could not understand why George would do such a thing. George seemed so happy. He was trusted. He did what he was told, and he never complained. He was such a good slave, in fact, that the master had taken him down to Savannah, had even given him an undated pass. And then George disappeared.

As the story poured out of the boys, Quashee leaned back against a tree, steepled his hands as though praying, and gave a sly smile. "Old George has been wearing a mask for years—did you know that? All the while he was planning and plotting escape when the right time arrived."

Toby asked the question they all wondered about. "What does that mean—that Old George wore a mask?"

A broad grin etched the lines across Quashee's forehead and cheeks so they appeared to glisten. "Old George did and said what the master wanted to see and to hear. But Old George's mind was liberated all the while. He laid hi s plan and he waited. He knew the time would come when his body could be as free as his mind."

"But George is an old man," blurted Sam. "I don't want to be a slave until I am old!"

Quashee gave Sam a stern and serious look. "Better to be an old man free than a young man in chains. As *you* still are."

The young men exchanged glances, twisted their lips in a smile, and nodded their heads. Quashee had made a good point.

"Running away with no plan will only bring you to trouble. You will be no different from others who've run to another plantation or into the woods for a few weeks, then were captured or forced by starvation to return to their plantation." Quashee's stern look remained. "You will just be like the rest who run away without being true freedom seekers."

All the excitement had drained from the boys' faces. "Peter got 100 lashes and was put into a cage," Tom remembered.

" Joe got his leg cut off, " John added.

" And is that what *you* want?" asked Quashee.

" No!" they all shouted together.

Quashee nodded. "If your goal is to live a free life like me, never to return to being a slave, then set your goals higher, my friends. Set them on freedom. Plan for a successful escape, but be patient. Discipline yourself. Old George did all of these things, and now he is free."

The young men now looked solemn. Again Quashee cautioned them that the right time had to be chosen with care.

"That must be a time the slaves are all gathered but the overseer is gone or not watching," he said. "You must have at least a day's head start before he finds you are missing. Usually the best time to leave is on the slaves' day off, Saturday night or Sunday." He shook his finger. "The journey to Florida will be very long. Start collecting your food and tools now. Find clothes to change into that aren't slaves' clothes."

The young men were listening intently. Now they had something specific to do. Quashee lifted his arms above his head and then stretched them out as wide as he could. "Here is the next of your learnings. You must respect and become one with this forest around you. Nature can seem like an enemy, but it is truly your dearest friend. The trees, flowers, herbs, and animals all will help you to make a safe journey."

The young men looked puzzled again. "What do you mean?" Jack asked for them all.

"When you became one with all this"—Quashee pointed again to the forest—"you are invisible here. You will be able to walk and to live in these woods without leaving a trace. They will protect you."

That very night the new learnings began. The young men gathered leaves, moss, and branches, and covered themselves in greenery. Then they practiced standing silent and tall like the trees. For what seemed like hours, they muffled their sneezes and coughs, ignored itches, and let insects crawl on their skin. Soon they had learned to walk backward to cover their tracks, and to balance themselves as they walked on low-hanging tree limbs. Quashee also taught them how to make fires without smoke. Night after night, they dug holes, stripped bark from trees, and gathered up twigs. Night after night, they practiced covering the holes so no sign of a fire remained.

"We're becoming one with the forest!" Jack exulted as, tired and sleepy, they trudged back to the quarters. They knew it would feel like they'd just gotten to bed when the bell rang for them to go to the fields. Sometimes they had. So Quashee made an herb tonic to help fight fatigue, and a bark ointment to rub on their aching muscles.

It was all worth it. As tired as they were, the friends carried only one picture in their minds. They would be free. Like Quashee, and like Old George.

The Plan Takes Root

Each night the young men slipped into the woods for their learnings with Quashee, and each morning they went back to work in the fields. Every free moment was spent in scouting the quarters for the foods and tools for the journey: yams, salt pork, and vegetables. Corn meal for ash cakes, okra seeds for coffee, a knife and a hatchet and flint for starting fires.

When Jack decided it was time to confide in Aunt Sally, his hands were shaking. "Aunt Sally, I think—I decided—" He could barely go on.

"What is it, boy? Spit it out." Impatience showed on Aunt Sally's face. "What's itchin' your britches?"

Jack finally blurted the words he'd dreaded to say. "I'm going to run away, Aunt Sally. And soon." Then he flinched as Aunt Sally dropped her cornbread and sat up straight in her chair.

"Did I hear you right? *You?* Run away?"

"Yes, m'am."

Aunt Sally sprang out of her chair, grabbed Jack close, and hugged him tight. "Baby," she crooned, "I had you ever since dey sold your mammy an' pappy away, when you was only six or seven years old. So you know I will miss you. But I want you to be free, so ol' Aunt Sally will give you all the help she can. You can be certain of dat." As he had done when he was a small boy, Jack laid his head down on Aunt Sally's chest. "Thank you, Aunt Sally. Thank you for understanding. I love you."

Each day after that, Aunt Sally collected small bits food from the big house. Sometimes it was biscuits, sometimes it was fruit, sometimes it was leftover pieces of meat. But one night she returned to the quarters excited. "Baby, it's time! You gotta leave by Sat'day afternoon!"

"What?" Jack was startled. "Why then, Aunt Sally? Does the master know?"

"Not about you," she assured him. "The master and mistress gonna be gone to a weddin' at the Drake plantation. They won't be back 'til Monday. So you boys betta leave on Sat'day, soon's you come in from the fields."

"But what if the master asks where I am? What will you say?" Jack worried that he was placing Aunt Sally in danger. " Will he guess you're hiding something?"

"Don't worry 'bout me, chile. I go up to the big house Monday mornin', an' I be screamin' an' cryin', 'He gone, he gone!' I be in hysteria, an' the mistress, she'll come an' fan me an' tell me to sit down. Den the master, he be tryin' to make some sense outta what I be sayin', but I jus' keep on cryin' 'He gone, he gone. By the time dey calm me down, you a'ready be gone a good two days. No chile, don' you worry 'bout me." She grinned. "Now it time for you an' me to see Granny 'bout getting' you some protection roots."

I hugged Aunt Sally hard. The next night, I gathered my friends and we went to see Granny, the medicine woman. Granny was the most respected person in the quarters. She delivered the babies, took care of the sick, and did other mysterious things for the quarters that people whispered about. Granny also taught the children the old ways that came from Africa and told them never to forget them.

A small, round woman with a wide toothless smile, her head wrapped in a red bandanna, opened the door to their knock. "Come in, chillen," she welcomed them. "How you be, Sally?"

Granny's cabin was different from any they had seen. It had the sweet smell and warm feel of the woods. All along the wall, sitting on the floor were jars filled with what looked like dirt and leaves. Next to a doll dressed in red and wearing different colored beads, a candle burned in the corner.

As Aunt Sally and Jack and his friends settled down, Granny opened an old wooden trunk and pulled out five red flannel bags. "We needs one o' these for each of you chillen." Next she placed some of her jars on the table, reached in, and extracted a pinch of herb from each one. All the while, she mumbled to herself. "Let's see. A little bit of Life Everlasting to keep you strong and healthy. Need some Angelica root for protection, too. Dis here Gopher Dust will trouble dem slave catchers." She laughed. "How 'bout a little of dis hot-foot powder to keep dogs and slave catchers away? Let's finish it off with some John the Conquer to chew."

After adding a rock and a coin to each red flannel bag, Granny stopped to consider. "Well now, chillen, need just a little bit of yore hair for yore bag." Having collected these from each one of them, she lit a cigar and blew smoke into each of the bags. "Now chillen, you be safe from ebyting, won't be no hound, no slave catcher, no wild animal git you. Granny make yore journey safe."

Then followed what seemed like the longest week of any before for the friends. They had trouble sleeping and eating. They counted the days until Saturday afternoon. But finally it came. After their work in the fields, they raced back to the quarters, gathered their bundles, and scurried off to the woods to meet Quashee.

Quashee carefully checked every bundle. He gave each of them a new bow made from mulberry wood, a bowstring of twisted deer hide, and hardwood arrows. Then he hugged each of the young men one by one. "You have successfully completed your learnings," he told them. "I have watched you all very carefully. You each have your own special gifts and talents that will be needed as you embark on your journey. You are ready to begin yours live as free men. But there is one last thing that we have to do before you depart."

The young men eyed each other. *Why now? Please not another learning,* they were all thinking.

But Quashee simply called each of them to him in turn. He placed his hands firmly on each boy's shoulders, looked him straight in the eye, and bestowed on him a new name to match what each of them represented. "Toby, you are now Ugo because of your strength. Sam, you are Nebe because of your special gift of watchfulness. John , you are Achebe, the one who protects. Tom, you will be Okwill because of your faith and belief. And you, Jack will be Obi, for Obidimkpa, meaning a man with a strong and courageous heart, the man who is the leader of the freedom seekers."

It was the greatest honor that Jack could have imagined. He vowed to be worthy of his new name.

$500 Reward
Ran Away Five Negroes

Left plantation on Sunday night. 15-20 years of age. Wearing cottong jackets and breeches. Believed to be headed for Florida. Jack, near six feet, light complected, a smart fellow, possibly can read and write; Toby, 5 feet 8 or 9, very black, very stout, scar on chin, strong constitution; brothers Sam and John, very black, 6 feet tall. Sam very deceitful, known to thieve. John has scar on side of face and a back used to the whip. Tom, a yellow fellow, slight limp, very religious. I will pay the above reward for the apprehension and delivery to the plantation. It is desired that they receive sufficient correction on the way home. B. Silcox, Subscriber.

The friends walked steadily for the first day and night, not stopping to eat or sleep, and careful to follow their learnings. Nebe, with his gift for careful watching, walked ahead of the group to watch for slave catchers, always ready to imitate the bird whistle as an alert to trouble ahead. Achebe, walking backwards, brought up the rear, making sure every branch was left in place and sprinkling the red and black pepper concoction from Granny to cover their scent. They drank the tonic that Quashee had given them to keep their bone-tired bodies on the move.

By Sunday night, they were so tired, thirsty, and hungry they finally stopped. Now what they needed most was a good place to sleep. First they made a fire without smoke the way Quashee had taught them; they baked ash cakes, roasted yams, and made okra-seed coffee. Next, following Granny's orders, they scattered mullein to protect them from wild animals and sprinkled "goofer dust" around the whole campsite to keep other enemies away.

Each took his turn as sentry. Because by the next morning they would be found to be missing, they had to take every precaution. Five healthy and strong young Negroes—valuable property—gone. "How is the overseer gonna explain this?" they chuckled, picturing his dilemma. "You think he'll get the whip?" What they knew for sure was that both he and the slave catchers would instantly be on their trail with the hounds.

But dangerous as the situation was, it also felt like a great adventure.

They were free. They were no longer bound by the rules of the plantation. "Just think," they said to each other, "no bell to wake us or tell us to come in from the fields. We own *ourselves*, and our time is our own."

The journey itself was far from easy, however. Day after day they fought their way through tangled thickets and thorny briars, left beaten and scratched. Day after day, they were swarmed by mosquitoes, biting flies, and hornets. Day after day, they had to be on the lookout for snakes, alligators, and bears. And day after day, their food supplies dwindled.

"We must eat only enough to kill hunger," they decided. They also remembered their learnings: to eat what the forest provided. As much as they could, they ate berries, grapes, wild greens, chestnuts, and hickory nuts. Quashee was right: nature was their friend.

Without warning, the forest became black as night on the fifth day. Seconds later, lightning zigzagged through the trees, and sheets of rain beat down as if the sky was exploding. There was no time and no place to seek shelter.

The wind howled, tree-branches thrashed, limbs flew through the air. Nature seemed to be in a deadly duel with itself. The friends struggled to cover themselves with moss and palmetto fronds, but against the hard rain these were useless. So fierce were the winds that they could only huddle together, wrapping themselves around shrubs that were near the ground. For two long days and nights it went on, the harshness of the storm like the overseer's lash. Rain stung their backs, and wet fronds beat against their drenched clothing. When it finally stopped, they emerged, trembling and shocked, from their refuge. For a long while after, they sat in silence.

"What just happened?" Achebe asked.

Ugo blinked in the sunshine. "I thought we would surely die," he confessed.

"Me too," echoed Okwill. "How would my mother feel if she knew it was a storm and not a slave catcher that almost killed me?"

Nebe's complaint voiced everyone's thoughts. "My corn-shuck mattress felt better than this soggy ground," he grumbled.

Okwill lowered his voice to a whisper. "I miss the quarters already. There was a lot of love there. I never got to tell Liza good-bye. I miss that girl."

Ugo sighed. "Well, fellows, we're still alive. Seems like we don't have to worry about anybody seeing our smoke for awhile. Let's just hope we aren't going to be dinner for some wild animal. I'd rather starve—and I probably will."

Obi listened to these exchanges in silence, but he too thought back to the quarters. Would Aunt Sally be okay? Would the master believe her? He reminded himself that Aunt Sally was clever. She had kept her cabin by complaining of nightmares when she slept behind the kitchen in the big house. Yes, Aunt Sally would be alright.

His thoughts were interrupted by Achebe's next statement. "It's not too late to turn back," he pointed out. "If we return on our own, maybe the master won't be so hard on us."

The others nodded, seeming almost convinced. All except Okwill. "God protected us through the storm," he objected. "He will take us safely to Florida."

Ugo ignored this. "How many lashes do you think we will get if we turn back now?" he inquired of the others.

An image of Quashee's stern, scowling face streaked like lightning through Obi's mind. He almost heard Quashee's voice urging him to be the freedom-seeker he'd trusted to lead the others. "Keep their minds focused on freedom," it told him.

Obi stood up, his back straight, his arms crossed. "Oh yes, it would be so nice in our cabins right now—sitting in front of the fire, eating corn pone and syrup. Who wouldn't feel better than we do, cold, wet, and hungry as we are? We could be dancing the jig on Saturday night with the pretty girls." He paused. "But just think, my friends. We would still be *enslaved*." Obi scowled in a good imitation of Quashee. Don't you remember the others who left just like us and gave up hope after meeting some obstacle? They might have stayed away for a week, or a month, or even longer. But then they came back. And why? Because they gave up on freedom too soon." The boys shifted uneasily.

"Have you considered what the folks in the quarters will think of us when they learn that five strong, healthy young men were beaten by rain? What will people too old and too tired to seek the freedom they want so badly others say about that?" Obi shook his finger at them just like Aunt Sally. The young men hung their heads. "What do we owe to those back home in the quarters who helped us prepare for this journey? Our success is not for ourselves alone. It gives hope to all the other souls still in bondage—hope that one day, they too will be free. And don't forget this: our escape tells the master and overseer that while they may purchase our bodies and labor, they can't own our minds. Nobody does...except us."

The young men stared at the muddy ground. Obi could almost see them wrestling with the opportunity and the burden that Quashee's learnings had placed upon them. Obi pointed to each one in turn. "Who wants to face Quashee's wrath? Tell me now. Who wants to turn back and submit to being a slave again?" A silence both heavy and deep fell upon them. "Well? Who will make this journey to Florida with me?"

Each bowed his head. And each muttered, "*I* will." They would not give up after all. They would not go back with heads bowed to be lashed. Before being enslaved once again, they would die. Yes, the days ahead would be difficult. They were weak. Their food was ruined. They needed fresh water. And the first task of all was to find a safe place to dry themselves and their clothing.

Nebe climbed a tall tree. "Look! A small island!" And there it was that the boys laid out all they could salvage, including their clothes, in the warm sun to dry. Ugo and Obi rigged up a trap for a rabbit or an opossum to roast over hot stones. Okwill and Achebe picked wild greens and berries. They had survived the storm. They kept warm. They would eat. They would rest and get back their strength. They would reach Florida.

Crossing the River to Freedom

Finally, the young men passed the five rivers that Quashee described and came to the branch of the St. Mary River. They knew this was it because Quashee had told them which way it flowed. When they crossed it, they would finally be in Florida!

As the boys peered through the trees at the water, they saw boat traffic. "It is too dangerous to cross here," Obi decided. "We will have to walk west to search for the narrow turn of the river that Quashee told us about."

So the exhausted but now-hopeful group trudged along with their bundles. They had walked for a time when a sharp bird-call pierced the air. Achebe! Danger! They froze. The wind at their backs carried the sound of distant voices approaching. How could this be happening? They were so close to freedom! They had survived cold, hunger, bee stings, insect bites, and that terrible storm. Nothing had stopped them. And now...

His heart throbbing loud, Obi signaled the others to become trees. Quickly hiding their bundles, they went into action. They covered their brown bodies with moss and merged with the woods, stifling each breath, watching and waiting. Only their eyes gleamed fear.

But when the voices came close, they were not slave-catchers' voices. Instead the young men heard the sweet and melodious sounds of their own speech. Soon Achebe appeared, followed by six more freedom seekers: five men, and a woman heavy with child.

The young men expelled their held breath. Along with it went all their dreaded imaginings. As Obi stepped forward, extending his leafy arm in a greeting— *"Haa'ty wilcum tuh oonuh!"*—light and joy filled every heart.

The newcomers leaped back in amazement to see a tree come to life. The group embraced and patted each other on the back. Wide smiles covered each face. Then everyone broke into hearty laughter.

"E one ub we people!" shouted one of the men.

"We glad fa see oonuh!" said another.

"Uh wa'k tell uh agonize my bone," added a third.

Obi gathered pinecones and a pile of leaves to make a comfortable spot for the woman to sit. "When are you going down?" he asked.

"Mi go down soon," she whispered.

One of the men overheard them. *"De gal brab. E boun' fuh go."*

"Uh baig'um fuh gone." She smiled. *"Want me chil bawn free."*

So Chance, Dink, Kyah, Puddin, Sweet, and his wife Queen joined the band of freedom seekers. Eleven of them now.

When they reached the narrow turn of the river, they crossed. They were free! They danced in place and hugged each other as their faces beamed with the light of freedom. To celebrate, Queen prepared a mouthwatering meal of marsh hen, oysters, and cooter soup.

That night each of them slept the sleep of the free.

Freedom in the Seminole Village

The next morning, singing the bird calls that Quashee had taught them, the young men signaled the Seminole Indians. Soon they were surrounded by the Seminoles and by the Africans who had preceded them to the land of the free.

As they entered the Seminole village, Obi's eyes and mouth both flew open at the same time. It was a scene that he would never forget: Africans dressed like Indians freely walking about, no overseer on horseback prodding them with a whip. African women laughing and talking with Indian women. Children running around and playing.

And young men just like himself, sitting under the tree, being taught by an elder. So *this* was freedom.

He was distracted by the drifting aroma of a simmering meat and vegetable stew. From the big black pot on a fire in the center of the village, he and the others were invited to help themselves. After second and even third helpings of stew and sizzling roast venison, they sat back, held their stomachs, and grinned.

This is freedom, thought Obi. *All the good food we can eat.*

He soon found out the African freedom seekers had much in common with the Seminoles. "We too came to Florida seeking a better life," explained the micco who welcomed them. "We were part of the Creek nation, but because of wars and oppression we too had to leave our ancestral lands. Like you, we wanted to be a free people."

If the group placed themselves under the Seminole *micco's* protection, they learned, they would be slaves in name only. And that name meant they could not be returned to the plantation. Just as Quashee had promised, the Africans would live a life equal to that of their protectors. Their only cost was to pay an annual tribute of livestock and crops.

"Your people allied with us so as to benefit both," the Seminoles *micco* went on. "We want to keep the European settlers from taking our lands. You Africans, African Maroons as you've come to be called, want to preserve your freedom."

Obi and his group had not been long in the village when Quashee paid a surprise visit. "My young man with the courageous heart," he greeted Obi, "you now have your freedom. You have earned it."

"Quashee, we owe our freedom to you and your learnings!" Obi insisted.

"But you *followed* my teaching, young man. And you aren't finished yet. You must now prepare for a new set of learnings: how to adapt to your new free life. Watch carefully, and listen. Then you will be ready to lead your own settlement."

As usual, Quashee was right. There was much for them to learn; to plant maize, beans, and other Seminole crops. To plant those beautiful pumpkins that hung from the trees. And to make good use of the palmetto palm tree.

"From the stalk of the palmetto palm, we women make baskets and sieves," Morning Star told them. "From the trunks, the men make the frames for our houses. With the leaves, we cover our roofs. And from the stems we make twine and rope." She plucked a piece of tender new growth at the top of the plan. "This we bake or eat raw if we're in the swamps."

The new freedom-seekers concentrated on Morning Star's words. "This is a very special food for us," she went on, pointing to yellow pods that looked like big kernels of corn. "When we are forced from our camps by the soldiers and hide in the swamps, we survive on the root of this cootie palm. We grind it to flour to make bread."

"Bread from a palm tree?" Queen was excited.

"Yes. But be very careful to prepare it correctly or it will be poisonous." Then she showed the startled Queen how to safely wash, pound, strain, and collect the dried yellow flour.

In return, the freedom seekers taught the Seminoles new ways to grow crops and how to plant rice. Quashee gathered all the young men, both Seminole and African, for training in battle techniques he had learned as a warrior in Africa. Obi himself became a favorite of the *micco* in the village. After the *micco* had taught him the Indian languages of Hitchiti and Mikasuki, Obi became so fluent in them, along with his English and Gullah, that he became the *micco's* translator—what the *micco* called a "sense carrier."

For nearly a year Obi's group lived like this in the Seminole village, patiently waiting for enough new African freedom-seekers to arrive to establish their own village.

The Founding of Ogun Town

The band of emancipated Africans marched like a determined army in search of a new home. They could now easily be mistaken for Seminoles: the women in brightly colored dresses and strings of beads around their necks. The men in buckskin leggings, calico shirts, silver crescents, and bracelets.

After hours of walking and searching, they spied a shallow creek that wound alongside a thicket of woods. Slogging across the creek, the group cautiously entered the woods, chopping and slashing their way through tangled limbs and underbrush. To their amazement, a wide grassy plain lay beyond it, scattered with trees and bordered by a swamp.

"This is it! This is perfect!" shouted one of the men.

"Dis is de bes land for farming!" proclaimed another.

Obi acknowledged their shouts with a smile. "No one can attack us here easily," he added.

"Eben we gon hab trouble findin dis here place agin," joked Queen.

Whoops and hollers roared through the crowd, and applause erupted. Husbands lifted wives up and swung them around. Others linked arms and danced in circles. One group paraded the length of the plain waving outstretched hands. Ideas formed in their heads and leapt from their mouths:

"Some of de cabins dey kin be here, and odder ober dere."

"De granary kin be right here, in de middle of de village."

"Dere be space enough to plant three fields here!" rejoiced Queen. *"And iffen de debil come, we kin hide in de marsh."*

Obie rubbed his hands together and clasped his closed fingers as if praying. "So this is the site for our new settlement?"

"Yes!" came the thunderous, resounding reply.

"What shall we call our new village? I suggest Ogun, for the African spirit of the forest who has guided us to this place."

"Yes! Ogun Town! "roared the crowd.

So the village was given its name, for the Yoruba spirit of Ogun, patron of blacksmiths, hunters, and warriors. Day after day the men worked to construct cabins like those of the Seminole. The women began planting crops. They planted rice by a small pond nearby. They agreed on a hiding place for "swamp" food.

At the entrance to the woods, an animal skeleton—representing Aya, the African symbol of versatility, endurance, and single-mindedness—was placed as a sentry post. The now well-worn path through the woods was covered with brush to hide spikes and sticks underneath, coated with the poison powder of Chinaberries. The true path purposely led through the worst of the thicket, a constant reminder of the journey they'd already taken and the dangers that they still faced.

On the night the village was finished, the proud residents celebrated with prayers, song, and dance. Obi, appointed as leader, stepped forward; the others sat on pine benches in the village-center. "Today is a great day," he began. "We are now residents of Ogun Town. Our journey toward this moment has been long and difficult, starting with the voyages all of us made aboard slave ships. We have come from different parts and speak different languages. Who are we?"

"Ibo!" shouted some.

"Yoruba!" shouted others.

"Fanti! Ashanti!"

"Welcome to all of you, brothers and sisters! Today we must become one people, a new people. Let us take language and tradition from all of our pasts and make it one. Our freedom and the safety of our women and children must be our first priority. So let us forget old animosities and grievances. Let us remember the saying, 'A people with no unity are conquered with one club.' Let us unite as one to protect what we cherish our freedom."

The group roared in agreement. "We are in this foreign land, but we cannot forget Africa," shouted one. "We must build our village on the old ways," another agreed. "We must keep our religion, building an altar to

66

honor our African spirits. We must not forget our ancestors; they are our link to God."

Other voices joined in. "We must love and respect the land as we do in Africa and as our Seminole brothers do here. We must work together and share the fruits of our labor. We must respect our elders. We must teach our children the learnings."

Thus it was that the freedom seekers created a new people that night, a new society based upon their African past, yet also borrowing from their Seminole allies and their recent plantation experiences.

Life in Ogun Town

As soon as they settled in at Ogun Town, Obi began to provide the young men in the town with the learnings that Quashee had taught him. Sitting beneath the large oak tree, he folded his hands as if praying, the same manner gesture Quashee had used. Then he addressed the young men.

"Even though we have established our own village, we are still in danger. We must constantly be on guard for slave catchers and the militias who want to return us to slavery. The most important lesson that *you* must learn is how to protect the freedom and safety of the town. First and foremost, you must learn to become warriors, protecting the women and children from harm. I will instruct you in the ways of warfare taught to young warriors in Africa."

At the same time, across the square, Queen had surrounded herself with the young girls. Besides learning how to plant and harvest crops, she was also teaching them the even more important lessons about how to remain free. "If an alarm is sounded," she began, "you must quickly gather our 'swamp food' and belongings from where they are hidden so we can flee into the swamps to hide."

Over the young peoples' heads, Obi smiled at Queen and then to himself, remembering the many hours that he had spent in the presence of Quashee as a young man himself, sometimes impatient with the learnings, but later grateful to have them, now fully appreciating them for their importance to his freedom.

****

On the anniversary of the first year in Ogun Town, the residents celebrated with food, singing, dancing, and merriment. Then Obi raised his hands to quiet the crowd, directing them to the pine benches built especially for such community meetings.

"My people, on this day, we thank the Creator for our good fortune and the good life provided us. The land and water given to us by our Creator belongs to us all. No one in Ogun Town lacks food, shelter, or clothing. The needs of everyone here met."

The men rose from the benches, heads raised, chins held high and chests thrust out. The women gave satisfied smiles and clapped loudly. Men and women saluted each other with bowed heads and clasped hands.

"We are blessed," Obi went on, "with good land, three fields filled with maize, cassava, squash, beans and other nourishing vegetables. Many of us own herds of horses, or cattle, or flocks of fowl. Our granary overflows. We have more than enough left over to give the micco, and to store as swamp food. We are working together in the African way: each aware that 'I am' because 'we are.'"

"Yes, yes!" the crowd shouted. "Tell us more!"

Obi spread his arms as if to embrace all of the children sitting in front on the ground. "Our children belong to the entire village. Our little girls learn from the women how to cultivate plants. Our little boys learn from the men to become warriors. Each one of us works for the good of the village; some are carpenters, some build canoes, some make pottery, some weave baskets. All we lack is a blacksmith. We must emancipate one from a plantation."

The crowd laughed and cheered. "A blacksmith must be liberated!"

Obi grew serious once again. "We love and respect our elders, who administer justice in the presence of the whole village. We do not have thieves because every person has enough." His eyes sparkled with pride. "Because we know the danger outside of our village, all of our people are guardians and protectors of the freedom that belongs to us all. For all of this, let us thank the Creator, and honor our African spirits and our ancestors for our good life in Ogun Town!"

The crowd jumped to its feet and cheered Obi again for his speech. "Let the celebration continue! More dancing, more singing, more palm wine!"

They celebrated well into the early morning. Obi thought of Aunt Sally. How he wished that she too could enjoy the freedom she had helped him to find.

For four peaceful years the people of Ogun Town lived a comfortable, plentiful life in the village.

Fighting For Freedom

The sun shone brightly, the trees blew gently in the breeze, and scattered clouds floated in the blue sky. The children placed flowers and offerings of spicy foods on the altar for Ogun and the ancestors, and then scampered off to play. As the women stirred pots of sofkee, worked in gardens, or sat in groups talking and weaving baskets, men tended the livestock.

Suddenly the alarm sounded. "Vacate the village! Vacate the village! Soldiers coming!" gasped the exhausted runner, falling into the square.

The village jolted into action. Panicked children raced back to their cabins, grabbed their swamp bags, and gathered in the center of the village. Fearful but determined women gathered swamp food from the emergency storehouse.

"Hurry! Hurry! There is no time to waste! The soldiers are coming!" Anxious young men rushed them all into the swamps, pushing the slow ones along. " Faster, faster!"

At the same time, village men streamed out in different directions to complete the tasks they had trained for. "Scatter the horses and cows! Shush! Shush! Git outta here!" Confused animals raced everywhere.

"Burn de cabins! Git a good one burnin on the granary! Leave nothing for dem debils to have!" Soon fires burned everywhere. Only the village altar of Ogun, the warrior spirit, was spared.

Thus the African Seminole Maroons deserted their homes. Fields full of vegetables, their horses, pigs and cows, cribs filled with corn—every precious possession acquired over the last four years—all were abandoned. The people's freedom was all that mattered. As they had been instructed, the warriors marched in front and back, and in the center in single file, were the women, children, and old people all carrying provisions into the refuge of the swamps.

Deep in the swamps, Obi finally spoke. "The time of war of which Chief Abraham warned has come upon us, the time when the government wants to send the Seminoles out west to what they call Indian Territory. But the Seminoles refuse to go, so they will do battle. If they lose and are sent away, the planters will want to enslave us again."

"No, no!" protested the group. "We will never again be enslaved! No man here will ever return to toil for another!"

Everyone joined in the shouting. "No man here will let his women, and his children born free, be enslaved!" They raised their fists in defiance. "We will fight until there is no more breath in our bodies!"

Soon messengers came from African Seminole Chief John Caesar saying that men were needed to raid the plantations in East Florida. Obi and half of the men of the village joined the raiders. Others remained to protect the women and children.

This was Obi's first battle, and he was energized. On each plantation the warriors raided, the men and women enslaved there cheered them on. Then they painted their own faces, grabbed guns, ammunition, axes, and hatchets, and joined the raiding parties.

One special newcomer excited the warriors: Mingo the blacksmith. With him came all the tools and materials needed to make weapons.

"Burn the fields!" yelled the raiders. "Torch the big house! We are the masters here now!"

And as they marched from plantation to plantation they chanted a battle hymn: "We are free, we are free!"

Meanwhile, life in the swamps became hard as the villagers moved from hamlet to hamlet searching for safety. They had to survive on the "famine food": coontie, wild berries, and greens from the woods. Each time they established a new village, the soldiers found them.

****

The American soldiers called this period The Second Seminole War, but Obi and his village knew that it was their war. It was a war to preserve the freedom and independence of Africans who had liberated themselves from enslavement. The war started in 1835 and lasted for seven long years. During those years, Obi and the men from his village fought valiantly employing all of the tactics of African warfare that they had learned from Quashee.

Finally, the African Seminole Chief Abraham sent word that a treaty had been signed that allowed them to emigrate safely to Indian Territory in the West. Like many others, Obi was bitterly disappointed. By the time he appeared before the village council, however, he was resigned. "If we surrender to the U.S. Army," he told them, "General Jesup has promised us freedom. We will not be separated from our families, or sold, or sent against our wills to Indian Territory."

The council agreed that it was best for them all to emigrate freely to the Indian Territory out West. They had fought bravely for many years, now they were displaced and starving. Obi made plans for the people of his own village. They traveled in wagons and on foot to Tampa Bay; there vessels were waiting to take them to Indian Territory in what is now Oklahoma.

But the new life out West was far from perfect; they were still pursued by slave-catchers determined to re-enslave them. Weary as they all were from moving—to Oklahoma, then to Texas—Obi was nevertheless determined to keep his people safe.

"We are no longer safe in the United States," Obi addressed his village council. "Therefore Chief John Horse will lead us to Mexico, where we can again be free. We must gather our arms and ammunition."

Queen, who by now had now become a leader of the women, stood up next. "We must be ready to leave as soon as possible. We will gather our dried pumpkin, our parched corn, and our smoked meat for the journey."

So the villagers packed up their horses for their next journey to freedom. All the food, tools, weapons, ammunition, and cooking utensils reminded Obi of the trip he had taken almost twenty years ago now. *But this time,* he thought, *we are facing bitter cold rather than tropical storms. Again we will be hungry and go without sleep. Again we will huddle in brush arbors and eat sofkee. And again the men will catch rabbits and squirrels.* Obi smiled to himself. But this time it will be our children who forage for edible plants.

As he had done years ago with his little band of freedom seekers, Obi spoke to his village. Older, more confident now, he raised his fists. "This trip will test our courage and dignity as a free people. We will not turn back. We must cross a river to safety a second time. This time it will be the Rio Grande, known to our people as the Rio Bravo." He paused. "The Freedom River."

Obi and his village crossed the Mexican border in 1850.

Years ago he had made the decision that he would never again be enslaved. Obi was true to himself. Every decision he made was to ensure the good life of freedom himself and the people in his village.

Epilogue

"When he was 105 years old, Obi died in Mexico. A drum beat informed the village that their leader was dead. His body was bathed and dressed in ceremonial attire: his buckskin leggings, long white shirt, vest, silver crescents, silver bracelets, beaded sash, and pouch.

The men in the village made a pine box coffin and dug Obi's grave. His body was reverently placed on a wagon pulled by his favorite horse and brought to the gravesite. The villagers walked behind in a silent procession. The casket was lowered into the ground, facing east. Overcome with grief, the villagers paid great tribute to him. "He was their hero."

At the time of his death, Obi was considered a rich man. He owned many head of cattle and herds of horses, on a large ranch with fields that overflowed with good crops. Yet not even one villager praised him for his wealth; they spoke only of his self-worth, self-dignity, and wisdom employed for the good of the village.

"Obi's mind was liberated," they said. "He was a free man."

"Obi respected himself and had self-dignity."

"Obi worked hard. He was a disciplined man."

"Obi was one smart fellow. He learned the ways of the Seminole. He spoke many languages."

"Obi honored his ancestors and his African heritage."

"Obi loved his village. He used his gifts and talents for the good of us all."

"Obi was a great leader! We all miss him!"

With these words, the old man, named Obi for his great-great grandfather and dressed as an African Seminole warrior, concludes his story. In his audience are children, youth, and adults, all sitting by now on the edge of their seats, their eyes fixed on the old man. Even the very young children are breathless and still. Like all spellbinding storytellers, he has taken them to a long-ago, faraway place that now feels as real as the hard chairs beneath them. So real that they almost don't want to come back.

On such Saturday evenings, the ramshackle house of this old warrior comes alive with adventure, daring, and courage. Because here, in the middle of an open field on John's Island, South Carolina, Obi tells his stories. Just outside, a garden decorated with blue bottle trees and colorful gourds welcomes all visitors.

The fire had burned low. It was almost time to go home. But the old man wasn't quite finished. "All of Obi's five children were born as free Africans. Like you." He gazed at each face in the audience. "After the Civil War and the end of slavery, his grandson, my great-grandfather, came back to the United States. Because I was given the name of this great man and hero, "Obi" it is my duty and honor to tell his story along with that of the self-emancipated Africans, the Maroons."

The old man paused. Then he stretched out his hands to the young people. "Why do *you* think it's so important to do this?"

The hands of several flew up. "Because they were heroes."

"Because they wanted to be free."

"Because they wouldn't give up trying to be free."

Old Obi smiled. "Yes, you are all right. Enslaved people could win their freedom only if the slave master or the government gave it to them by emancipating them. But the Maroons freed themselves; they self-emancipated. They lived near the Seminole Indians and fought alongside them. But they established their own villages, basing them on the old African ways. In their special way, the Maroons won a victory over the institution of slavery."

The old man pushed himself up from his chair and picked up his musket. "It is now time to go. But remember: it's important that the Maroons' story be told". And as quietly as Quashee had entered his great-great-grandfather Obi's life, the old man left the room.

****

The stories that Obi the elder tells are the "untold history", history that none of us learn in school--stories about the Africans who resisted enslavement, who did *not* accept it willingly, who ran away determined to make their own destinies. The stories are "untold" because those who teach social studies and history have not heard them either. How few people, teachers included (and their teachers too) have ever even heard of the Maroons? How many are even vaguely aware of the courageous and powerful role they played in the history of Florida and of the United States?

Now, however, you who read this story *are* hearing about them. Now you can tell the story of the Maroons to others, since *you*—the storytellers of today—are the ones with this knowledge. You, like Obi himself, can carry forward a proud tradition of courage and power.

OBI

LEADER OF OGUN TOWN

Our Hero

1815-1920

Glossary

Cooter: a river turtle with a brown shell and yellow stripes on the head

Cootie Palm: a palm tree native to Florida; an important food source for the Seminole Indians; coontie means "flour root". Later known as "arrow root" when plants south Florida produced starch from the root.

Gullah: descendants of enslaved Africans who live on the Sea Islands, and the coastal regions of North Carolina, South Carolina, Georgia, and Florida. The Gullah have preserved much of their African cultural heritage. Also called CooterGeechees.

Gullah Language: language spoken by the Gullah people with strong influences from West African languages.

Hitchiti/Mikasuki Languages: languages spoken by the Seminole people.

Micco: Seminole leader or chief

Sieve: a mesh utensil used for straining solids from liquids

Sofkee: a thin mush or porridge made from corn meal

Appendix

Seminole Maroon Leaders

Obi was a clearly a hero himself, but like many wise and good men, he had heroes of his own—African Seminole Maroon chiefs he looked up to and emulated.

Abraham

Abraham escaped slavery in Pensacola as a young boy and fled to the Seminoles. He became a prominent African Seminole leader during the Second Seminole War.

Abraham was referred to as "Yobly" by the Seminoles because of his intelligence and influence, and was given the name "Prophet" by his fellow African Seminoles.

Abraham's military career began in 1814 when he was one of the African slaves fighting for the British during the War of 1812. Abraham also fought and escaped from the Negro Fort when it was destroyed in 1816. It was in the Battle of the Suwannee that Abraham gained the recognition and trust reserved for Seminole warriors. He became a slave (placed himself under the protection) of Micanopy who had become principal Chief of the Alachua. As a member of the Seminole community gained the titles of interpreter, spokesman, sense-bearer, and chief advisor to Chief Micanopy.

Abraham served as interpreter and counselor for Chief Micanopy in 1832 meeting at Payne's Landing between the U.S. government and the Seminoles to negotiate passage to Indian Territory in the west. Abraham realized that there were no provisions made for African Seminoles and that they would be returned to enslavement. When he accompanied the delegation of chiefs to inspect the land planned for Seminoles in Arkansas, Abraham began to devise a plan which would mean that African Seminoles would obtain land and live free.

Abraham was the most dominant leader opposed to Seminole emigration. Abraham was able to demonstrate to the Seminoles that the plight of the African Seminoles was related to that of Native Seminoles. A common and inseparable bond was formed and the two groups took a unified stand against emigration to Indian Territory in the west.

Abraham gave U.S. authorities the impression that he was in favor of enforcing the treaty while he prepared for war. He received shipments of gun powder and other arms from Cuban fishermen and secretly notified Africans on plantations to revolt when the war broke out.

Abraham was involved in the Second Seminole War from its beginning; during the first two years, he was heavily involved in fighting, strategic war planning, and negotiations. Abraham knew that ultimately the Seminoles could not prevail in a war against the United States because of the power and wealth of the U.S., so he planned /a long guerilla war that would force U.S. political and military leaders to alter the treaty to provide better terms for Africans. He developed a "hit and run" strategy designed "to fly before the army and avoid battle" taking refuge in the dense swamps and hammocks of the Everglades.

Abraham consistently interpreted and counseled with the interests of his people, the African Seminoles in mind. Abraham sought either the right to remain in Florida or free passage for all Africans among the Seminoles to Arkansas and land separate from the Creeks. His plan worked. Abraham negotiated the right of Africans to be granted free passage to Indian Territory among the Seminoles.

In 1839, Abraham himself left Florida along with his family and 90 other African Seminoles. In 1850, Abraham was among the Black Seminoles who migrated across Texas into Mexico. Abraham was a leader and an abolitionist. Freedom for himself and his people was a lifelong struggle for Abraham.

John Caesar

The child of runaway slaves, John Caesar lived most of his life among the Seminoles. He was a "slave" of Chief Emathla, the principal chief of the St. John's River Seminoles. Caesar became Emathla's counselor and interpreter. He was also commander of the African Seminoles under Emathla's protection.

Caesar was next to Abraham in influence and importance among African and Native Seminoles.

During the Second Seminole War, Caesar was a primary instigator of the plantation slaves, a principal leader of plantation raids, interpreter, negotiator, diplomat, and overall African Seminole leader. Caesar was responsible for establishing ties between African Seminoles and plantation slaves.

John Caesar's wife was enslaved on a plantation. He visited her and several other plantations in the area frequently. Caesar provided those still enslaved on plantations a model of freedom; he came and went as he pleased while being a "slave" of a Seminole. Caesar met with leaders of the slave community and as a result influenced the enslaved population in general.

The most significant contribution of John Caesar was his ability to unify the Seminole cause with Africans on plantations and to provide leadership to those who joined him. He incited and inspired many of the enslaved to no longer tolerate life in bondage.

In 1835, John Caesar assumed a leadership position and led the attacks upon plantations located around the St. John's River. The destruction of plantations caused both economic woes and aided the recruitment of slaves. Once the enslaved witnessed the resistance of the Native and African Seminoles, they became very motivated in securing their own freedom. Runaway slaves painted their faces as a symbol of their allegiance to the Seminole cause.

Caesar inaugurated a guerilla campaign primarily utilizing runaway slaves. Without the assistance of slaves and free Blacks, the Seminole cause would not have been as successful.

John Cavallo

John Cavallo, also known as Gopher John and John Horse served the longest length of time in war and was the U.S. military's greatest adversary. Born in 1812, he was the son of Seminole Chief Charles Cavallo and an African woman. John grew up near Tampa Bay, close to Lake Thonotosassa.

John got the guerre "Gopher John" because at about 14 years of age, unknowingly to the officers at Fort Brooke, he sold the same two gophers time after time and collected a quarter each time. The soldiers discovered his prank and jokingly called him "Gopher John".

During the period 1835-1836, John became an African Seminole war chief known throughout the Florida territory. He was the African Seminole leader most active in efforts to unify African Seminoles and the plantation slaves on Florida's western frontier.

In the west, John Cavallo would be known as "John Horse". He was given the war name "Hokepis Hejo or Crazy Breast" as an honorary war title meaning that "his heart is recklessly brave". As he had in the Second Seminole War, John Horse's mission was to seek freedom for his people. African Seminoles continued to face hardships and the possibility of re-enslavement in the west. As a result of the leadership of John Horse, African

Seminoles would receive more security and freedom in Oklahoma and Texas. He went on to found an African Seminole settlement in Nacimiento, Mexico.

To African Seminoles in the west, John Horse became their politician, ambassador to the United States and Mexican governments.

John Horse also became a doctor to his people. He mastered the art of tribal medicine and provided his people with herb healing remedies.

John's life represented one of leadership and dedication to his people. Within one year, he was elevated from sub-chief to war chief. His role as Chief Alligator's sense-bearer and principal advisor gained him the respect of both the Seminoles and the U.S. Government. John was a negotiator, advisor, and commander. Without the military strategy of John Horse and his willingness to wage war, African Seminoles may very well have been re-enslaved.

Discovering My Heroes

As a young boy growing up in a 1950's small town setting, my heroes were the American cowboy stars. Every Saturday evening we made a beeline to what we called in those days the "picture show". It was always exciting to see them on the big silver screen bringing law and order to the Territory; fighting against the clutches of evil men. They championed the cause of those treated unjustly. Yes, indeed they were the ones we called heroes. I guess growing up we did not have the concept of what a true hero should be; even though these men may have been fictitious characters.

Just a few years ago, I learned about true heroes within my own family. The story begins with my great-great grandfather. He and his family ran away from slavery in Alabama to live with the Seminoles in Central Florida. They were African Seminole Maroons. For my great-great grandfather to escape degradation, and tyranny and to set a course to freedom for his family in those dangerous and trying times was truly heroic. He came to a new land, hued out a living for his family. After generations my family survived and we are still here. As some would say through "Divine intervention".

I'm here today to tell the old stories of courage and perseverance of these people who are my heroes.

John Griffin performs African Seminole Maroon re-enactments of the 1800's Seminole Wars.

Selected Sources

1. Blyden, Edward W., *African Life &*
   *Customs,*Baltimore, Maryland: Black Classic
   Press, 1908.
2. Dixon, Anthony, *Black Seminole Involvement and*
   Leadership During the Second Seminole War
   1835-1842, Doctoral Dissertation, 2007.
3. Franklin, John Hope and Schweninger, Loren,
   Runaway Slaves: Rebels on the Plantation, New
   York: Oxford University Press, 1999.
4. Geraty, Virginia Mixon, *Gulluh Fuh Oonuh (Gullah*
   For You): A Guide to the Gullah Language,
   Orangeburg, South Carolina: Sandlapper
   Publishing Co., 2006.
5. Gottlieb, Karla. *The Mother of Us All: A History of*
   Queen Nanny- Leader of the Windward
   Jamaican Maroons, Trenton, NJ: Africa World
   Press, 2000.
6. Guinn, Jeff, *Our Land Before We Die: The Proud*
   Story of the Seminole Negro, New York: Jeremy
   P. Tarcher/Penguin, 2002.
7. Littlefield, Daniel , *Africans and Seminoles.* Westport:
   Greenwood Press,1977.
8. Katz, William Loren, *Breaking the Chains: African*
   American Slave Resistance, New York:
   Atheneum, 1990.

9. Mitchell, Faith, *Hoodoo Medicine; Gullah Herbal Remedies,* Columbia, South Carolina: Summer House Press, 1999.

10. Mock, Shirley Boteler, *Dreaming with the Ancestors: Black Seminole Women in Texas and Mexico.* Norman, Oklahoma: University of Oklahoma Press, 2010.

11. Mulroy, Kevin, *Freedom on the Border: The Seminole Maroons in Florida, the Indian Territory, Coahuila, and Texas,* Lubbock, Texas: Texas Tech University Press, 1993.

12. Porter, Kenneth W., *The Black Seminoles: History of a Freedom-Seeking People,* Gainesville: University of Florida Press, 1996.

13. Reid, Vic, *Nanny Town.* Kingston, Jamaica: Jamaica Publishing House Limited, 1983.

14. Thompson, Alvin O., *Flight to Freedom: African Runaways and Maroons in the Americas,* Kingston, Jamaica: University of the West Indies Press, 2006.

Facilitator Training

The Maroons:
Lessons in Courage and Character Curriculum

The Maroons: Lessons in Courage and Character Curriculum consists of the book, *Obi: Seminole Maroon,* *and the Obi: Seminole Maroon Workbook.*

The workbook provides discussion questions and activities that promote personal growth and character development. It includes individual and group projects, i.e., establishing a Maroon garden, foraging for native plants and edible foods, conducting research, writing poetry, short stories, plays, creating replicas of Maroon villages, etc. The curriculum provides the opportunity for participants to engage in positive peer group interactions, learn untold history, explore new experiences, engage in community service projects, develop leadership skills, gain entrepreneurial knowledge, and discover/develop personal gifts/talents.

Training is available for parents, community volunteers, community police officers, youth workers, teachers, counselors to implement the curriculum with middle school students. Also, high school (juniors/seniors) and college students can become trained to facilitate the curriculum with middle school students to earn service learning credits.

For Information Contact:

biredagrp5@aol.com or call (941)639-2914.

Coming Soon:

The Maroons: Freedom Fighters of the Americas

Expand your knowledge of the Maroons. Learn about the feats and triumphs of such freedom fighters as Nanny, Zumbi, Maceo, Bayano, and St. Malo in this exciting new book, available in 2014.

CPSIA information can be obtained at www.ICGtesting.com
Printed in the USA
LVOW01s0834010714

392465LV00004B/8/P